D0575885

UNCLE JAMES

UNCLE JAMES

BY *Marc Harshman*

ILLUSTRATED BY *Michael Dooling*

COBBLEHILL BOOKS · Dutton/New York

Library of Congress Cataloging-in-Publication Data
Harshman, Marc. Uncle James /
Marc Harshman ; illustrated by Michael Dooling.
p. cm.
Summary: As a young boy and his family endure hard times
on their Indiana farm, they look forward to the letters
and promises of help from their uncle out west.
ISBN 0-525-65110-1
[1. Uncles—Fiction. 2. Farm life—Fiction.]
I. Dooling, Michael, ill. II. Title.
PZ7.H256247Un 1992 [Fic]—dc20 92-2660 CIP AC
Published in the United States by Cobblehill Books,
an affiliate of Dutton Children's Books,
a division of Penguin Books USA Inc.,
375 Hudson Street, New York, New York 10014
Designed by Kathleen Westray
Printed in Hong Kong First Edition
10 9 8 7 6 5 4 3 2 1

For Margaret and Jack.
M.H.

For Patricia Dooling, my mom, whose support
and guidance made this book possible.
M.D.

He was my uncle—my mother's brother who had moved out west. "High in the western mountains," wrote Uncle James.

We live in Indiana. Here it is flat and we raise chickens and wheat. And our father is dead. It took a while before I could say that, but growing up with it this past year, I've learned to.

Uncle James wrote that he was going to help. We needed it that winter. We were hungry, the baby sick, and all of us tired from trying to keep the farm going. And, of course, we all missed Father. Finally, I had to quit school to help out. Mother said that with the baby to look after, Anna and Lizabeth might have to leave school, too. But I told her that, no, Uncle James would be here soon and everything would be fine.

We looked forward to his letters. He wrote he was making real good money in the logging camps. He also told us great stories about life out west.

"Listen to what his letter says today, children," Mom said. " 'I got done early today. I had to kill two rattlesnakes outside my cabin. But that didn't take long. Then I got a bear with my old shotgun and brought it back to camp for supper.' "

Another day we got a postcard.

"The canyon in this picture was filled to the top with water yesterday, a real, raging river it was. We've had 30 inches of rain. I had to row to camp, but I'm doing fine and still making money. I'll send some soon. Love, Uncle James."

"Oh, isn't he the best uncle ever?" Lizabeth declared. We all nodded our heads, imagining a world so different than our own.

It seemed like just yesterday a letter had said: "Great day in the morning! After I cut and stacked fifty giant pine trees, I started walking back and what should greet me but a mountain lion! I only had my axe but I aimed real good just as he leaped and oh, you should see the pretty rug I'm bringing you home, Sister. And a cap for Jimmy. And tell the girls not to worry, I got surprises for them, too!"

Such stories and promises of help sure helped brighten our evenings. I could hardly wait for Uncle James to come. But otherwise things did not look so bright. We made it through the winter, but my sisters had to leave school early. They were a big help planting the fields after Mom or I had plowed.

Mother said to pray that Uncle James would be coming real soon. She wrote to him, but we didn't know what she said. On a postcard that came one day was a picture of a man on top of a forty-foot spruce with all its limbs chopped off. Uncle James said it was him in the photo. He also said he'd better not send money through the mail because it might get lost. He'd bring it himself, which wouldn't be long now.

Summer came, and we all worked harder than ever. Our neighbor Mr. Landscomb said I was becoming a real man, but I knew I was still a boy and not a man like Father had been, nor one like Uncle James.

It was not easy for Mother with a baby and three other children to run a farm on her own. We worked from sunup to sundown, all of us but the baby who was work himself. I took a turn watching him sometimes. "Boy, I wish I knew a potion that would make you a grownup." We needed help. Someone. Uncle James?

That summer we had plenty to eat because our garden was good. We thought we might even make enough from the wheat we had raised to come out with a little extra. Mr. Landscomb said he'd thresh our wheat for free since I'd helped him with his hay. But then the end of summer turned dry and we began to worry if we'd have even as much as last winter. We all knew we had had just barely enough then. We hoped and prayed that Uncle James would come soon.

And he did, knocking at the door late one September night. Before we could get down the stairs, Mom yelled up, "You all stay in bed. Everything's okay."

But we had heard—his voice, and heard Mom say, "James Goodman, you're drunk!"

I think we all tried not to hear that last part. "But, Mom, we want to see Uncle James. We've waited so long."

"No! Do as I say. Your uncle is tired and wants to rest. Now, hush."

In the morning we met Uncle James. Well, sort of. He didn't sit at the table with us. He was in the big rocking chair in the corner, looking out the window. He looked awful—his eyes bloodshot. He didn't look like a strong, brave, successful logging man at all. Mom tried to get us out to our chores as quickly as she could. I tested her, though, by going over and saying, "Good morning, Uncle James."

"G'day, young Jimmy," he replied with a weak smile.

So, Uncle James had come. But he didn't bring any money, nor any lion rugs or hats or any surprises. Only disappointment.

That evening he joined us at table and told us what we'd already guessed, that his letters were mostly lies. It wasn't a confession that any of us wanted to hear. I think he wanted us to feel sorry for him. I didn't.

Mom said later that we were lucky. At least he didn't bring any debts. She didn't mention that she and Father had loaned him the money to go west.

Mom also said we still could use help. It would be up to Uncle James whether he was to be that help or not. I told Mom I hated him and I wished he would leave and that Anna and Lizabeth felt the same and that we could get by somehow. Mom said that she agreed we would get by, somehow. She said the important question was whether Uncle James would get by.

"Uncle James! Why should we care? He didn't care about us. All he did was lie to us and lead us on and take money from you and Dad. He's just an old drunk!"

"You're right, and you're wrong, Jimmy. He did make up stories. He built our hopes up horribly, and yes, borrowed some money from your father. But he did care about us, too. His words lied, but his heart didn't. He wanted the best for us even if he couldn't make those things happen. He really didn't have to write those letters. And weren't they great evenings just imagining those things he said? Uncle James is a good storyteller, but he got sidetracked. The hardest story to tell is the one about ourselves because that's the one we have to tell true."

Well, Uncle James' story isn't finished yet. He's been here six weeks now and isn't drinking, and that's good. How Mom did it, I don't know, but she did. There have been a lot of long talks at night, about our grandparents and lots of things I don't really understand. I think she argued with him and stood up to him and listened to him and loved him. He needed them all.

Mom says it's an ache like a sickness that hangs on a man a long time and that it will be a long time before he's well. But he is getting better and is a big help to us. He can scythe twice as fast as Mom or I, and already has all the winter wood cut and laid by. Even if he is sometimes awful quiet, he can be cheerful and funny, too. And he sure makes the work go faster with all his jokes and memories of life out west.

After supper he sits down and tells us wonderful tales. He tells us the real true stories of life in the west, not just about rattlesnakes and mountain lions. Before bedtime he'll tell us the stories that we know aren't exactly true, the tall tales men told him around the campfires, about men named Paul Bunyan and Pecos Bill.

I still remember how much the disappointment had hurt when those stories in his letters turned out to be untrue. I guess that's just the way some people are—making up stories to make real life seem better than it is. Mom says that's okay, as long as he remembers that he's the teller of the story and not the story itself. She says he knows again what's a true story and what's a story story.

But what's best, Mom says, is that we're all learning to help Uncle James with a new story, the one in which he can be the hero.

And we all still need heroes, even ones like Uncle James.